THE ANGEL of NITSHILL ROAD

Anne Fine

Illustrated by
Garry Wing

Series Editors
Steve Barlow and Steve Skidmore

The Angel of Nitshill Road

Nitshill Road School is at the scruffy end of town. There's nothing special about it, except that the bully Barry Hunter makes life miserable for plump Penny, clumsy Mark and shy Marigold. Then one day a perfect stranger appears at the gates. Celeste is new. She's bright as fresh paint. And she's extraordinary. Celeste brings a book to school – an empty book she calls the Book of Deeds – in which she writes down every spiteful thing that Barry Hunter does. Can she be the Recording Angel, as Marigold and some of the others believe? Or is she just sick of watching the bullying?

Either way, when she gives Mr Fairway the book, he can't pretend any longer that he doesn't know what's going on in his own class. Everything's going to change.

And then Celeste disappears. But where's she gone?

The Main Characters

Celeste
Celeste comes out of the blue – bright, cheerful and super-confident. Everything about her glows, from her snow-white dress to her shop-shiny shoes. Her voice is clear as a bell. She seems rather old-fashioned in some ways.

Barry Hunter
Barry's a typical bully – wrapped up in himself, rushing about. He doesn't realise how mean he's being to other people. He thinks it's all a good laugh.

Penny
Penny has to act like a big girl who's been made shy by a lot of teasing. When she's alone with her friends, she's fine. When Barry shows up, she goes quiet.

Mark
Mark's a bit silly and clumsy. He trips over his own feet. His hair sticks up in an odd way. He chews his fingers. His glasses are important to him, but keep falling off. He gets close to tears and tempers when he's pushed.

Marigold
Marigold is secretly terrified by Barry Hunter and school generally. She doesn't make friends. She only breaks through her shy shell when she sees Barry Hunter is being brought under control at last.

Mr Fairway
Mr Fairway is the class teacher. He means well enough, but he's busy. He's not the sort to take the time to find out what really happened. He can be irritable, too.

Celeste

Penny

Marigold

Barry Hunter

Mark

Mr Fairway

In the Playground
(*Starring: Barry Hunter the bully, Mark, Penny, Lisa, All-the-class, Celeste, Mr Fairway the teacher.*)

All-the-class: (*In a whisper chant*)
Here comes Barry Hunter,
Making people cry.
Who's he picking on today?
Poor old Penny!

Barry: Here I come. I'm a jet-fighter. Vroom-vroom. Out of my way, everyone. Oh, no! It's Penny, the Moving Mountain. She's too big to miss. I'm going to crash!

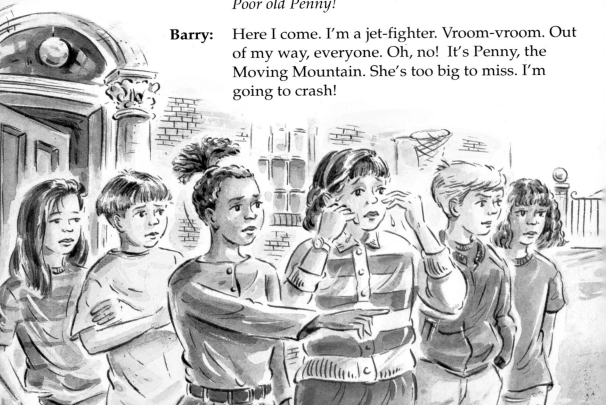

Penny: Go away, Barry. Leave me alone.

Barry: Moving Mountain! Moving Mountain!

All-the-class: (*Whispering*) Look, Penny's crying now.

Barry: I'm off. Vroom-vroom!

All-the-class: (*In a whisper chant*)
There goes Barry Hunter,
Making people cry.
Who's he picking on today?
Poor old Mark.

Barry: Where am I? I must have flown to Mars by mistake. Here's Mark the Martian. He's got strange sticky-up hair and glasses as thick as bottle ends. He can't be human.

Mark: Push off, Barry Hunter.

Barry:	He speaks! He can't catch a ball or save a goal, but he can speak!
Mark:	Go away. Leave me alone.
Barry:	Watch me poke the Martian. Look, he's getting mad. He's glaring through his bionic eyes. He's getting his controls in order. He's crashing his gears. He's getting ready to hit me! *(Mark lashes out.)* He missed!
	(Barry runs off.)
All-the-class:	*(Whispering)* Look, Mark's crying now.
Lisa:	They ought to tell.
All-the-class:	Tell who?
Lisa:	Penny's big sister.
All-the-class:	Guess what she'd say. *(Imitating a big sister)* "Just stay away from him. Then he won't bother you."
Lisa:	That won't work, then. How about Mark's big brother?
All-the-class:	Guess what he'd say. *(Imitating a big brother)* "If he hits you, just you hit him back!"
Lisa:	That isn't going to work. We could tell the caretaker or the dinner lady.
All-the-class:	Guess what they'd say. *(Imitating)* "You'll all have to learn to sort yourselves out."
Lisa:	Well, that won't work. What about telling Mr Fairway?
All-the-class:	Guess what he'll say. *(Imitating Mr Fairway)* "Really, Mark, you bring a lot of it on yourself."

Lisa:	We'll have to tell their mothers, then.
All-the-class:	Guess what they'll say. *(Imitating)* "I'm going up the school if it doesn't stop."
Mark & Penny:	It hasn't stopped.
Lisa:	But they haven't gone.
All-the-class:	Stuck!
Lisa:	Watch out! The gate's opening. Barry must be coming back.

(Enter Celeste.)

Penny:	It isn't Barry.
Mark:	It's a girl.
Lisa:	Look at her! White frock!
All-the-class:	White shoes.
Penny:	White socks.
All-the-class:	Clean hands.
Mark:	Sparkling hair.
All-the-class:	She looks like a perfect angel!
Celeste:	Am I in the right place? Is this Nitshill Road School?
Penny:	Are you new?
Celeste:	Absolutely! I'm shop-shiny new!
Lisa:	Have you come all by yourself?
Celeste:	My father was with me, but he had to fly.
Mark:	Where have you come from?

Celeste: (*Waving airily*) Oh, somewhere up there.

All-the-class: What's your name?

Celeste: Celeste.

All-the-class: Celeste!?!

Celeste: The name means "heavenly".

(*While they're all staring at her, Barry Hunter comes back.*)

Barry: Vroom-vroom! Watch out, little Miss Perfect, or I'll bump into you and spoil your lovely white frock. Vroom-vroom!

Celeste: What a rude boy. Was he born in a bucket?

Lisa: That's Barry Hunter. He's a horrible bully.

Barry: Vroom-vroom! I'm coming back. Get out of the way, Moving Mountain, or I'll hit you. Or are you too big to move?

8

Penny:	Go away, Barry Hunter! Stop being horrible. I can't help being fat. Leave me alone!
Celeste:	Is he horrid to everyone?
Lisa:	He can be. But most days he picks on Penny and Mark.
Celeste:	Which one is Mark?
Lisa:	The one he's picking on now.
Barry:	Let me see your new pencil box, Mark.
Mark:	Give it back! It's mine!
Barry:	Say please.
Mark:	It's my box. You snatched it. Give it back!
Barry:	Manners! Say please.
Mark:	Quick! The bell's ringing. Give it back. We have to get in line.
Barry:	Say please, and I might let you have it.
All-the-class:	Quick! Teacher's coming.
	(Enter Mr Fairway.)
Mark:	Please.
Barry:	Pretty pretty please.
Mark:	That isn't fair! Pretty pretty please.
Barry:	A bit louder. I can't hear you.
Mark:	*(Yelling)* Pretty pretty please!
Mr Fairway:	Who's making all that noise? Mark, is it you?
	(Celeste darts forward behind Barry Hunter.)

Barry:	Yeeouch! Ouch!
Mr Fairway:	Oh, it's Barry Hunter.
Barry:	She *bit* me! That new girl *bit* me! There! Toothmarks on my leg!
Mr Fairway:	What's going on? Who are you?
Celeste:	I'm the new girl. Celeste. And I bit him. Hard.
Mr Fairway:	But *why*?
Celeste:	Well, you can't like *everyone*, can you?
Mr Fairway:	This isn't a very good start, is it, Celeste?
Celeste:	Oh, you can tell me off. It's your job. But I warn you, don't do it so hard you make me cry. Once I start, I weep *buckets*.
Mr Fairway:	What an extraordinary child!
Lisa:	Be my best friend, Celeste.
Penny:	And mine.
Mark:	And mine.
All-the-class:	Be mine, too.
Barry:	Not mine! No thank you! Not mine!

> **Scene 2**
>
> **Behind the Lavatories**
> (*Starring: Lisa, Peter, Tracey, Penny, Stephen, Yusef, Elaine, Ian, Mark, Celeste, Barry Hunter, Mr Fairway, Half-the-class (1) and Half-the-class (2).*)

Lisa: I think Celeste is an angel.

Peter: Don't be silly.

Tracey: There's no such things as angels.

Lisa: Yes there are.

Penny: Who thinks there are really angels?

Half-the-class (1): I do!

Tracey: Who thinks there aren't?

Half-the-class (2): I do!

Stephen: She has an angel's name – Celeste.

Yusef: And she has an angel's voice. I heard Mrs Porter say so. "That new girl Celeste has a heavenly accent."

Elaine: And I heard someone in the office saying that she came right out of the blue!

Ian: And I heard Mr Fairway telling the head teacher yesterday that Celeste was having a bit of trouble coming down to earth!

11

Lisa:	See? She *sounds* like an angel.
Penny:	Remember when she said her father had to *fly*?
Stephen:	When Mr Fairway asked her if her chair was wobbling, she said, "Yes, but it's as comfy as a cloud."
Yusef:	How would anyone know how comfy a cloud is?
Elaine:	Unless they were a real angel ...
Penny:	She looks like all the angels that I've ever seen in paintings and films and books.
Lisa:	I think she *is* an angel.
Half-the-class (1):	Ssshh! Here she comes!
Half-the-class (2):	And here comes Barry Hunter!
	(Enter Celeste, with Barry behind her.)
Barry:	Today, I'm flying a bomber, but I can't get round this huge Penny Mountain because it's so big and fat!
	(Celeste puts out her foot as Barry comes by and trips him up flat on the ground.)
Barry:	Yeeeouch!
Celeste:	That's for calling Penny *fat*.
Barry:	Penny *is* fat.
Celeste:	And you're a horrible bully. But what you're too stupid to realize is that if Penny stopped stuffing her face with sweets and crisps all day, she'd soon be as thin as I am. But you're a horrible bully, and it's harder to change that. If you're not careful, Barry Hunter, no one will ever really like you.

Barry: At least I'm normal. Not like Mark, with his sticky-up hair and his funny walk.

Celeste: Leave Mark alone.

Barry: I don't know why you keep sticking up for him. He's *weird*.

Mark: I'm *not* weird!

Barry: Well, you're not *normal*, are you? *(Barry taps Mark's head.)* Helloooo! Helloooo! Is there anyone in there? No. You're not normal.

Celeste: And you are, are you?

Barry: Yes, I am.

13

Celeste:	Gather round, everybody! Gather round! We're going to do a survey. Who wants to be normal if normal's like Barry Hunter?
Half-the-class (1):	Barry Hunter is mean.
Half-the-class (2):	He's spiteful and horrid.
Half-the-class (1):	He steals things and hides things.
Half-the-class (2):	And makes people cry.
Half-the-class (1):	Then he says, "Only a joke! Only a game!"
Half-the-class (2):	He loves making people unhappy.
Celeste:	He *says* he's normal.
Tracey:	We'd all be happier if he wasn't here.
Stephen:	He ruins every lesson.
Ian:	He wastes time and puts Mr Fairway in a bad mood.
Celeste:	He *says* he's normal.
Elaine:	He spoils games.
Paul:	He teases people in the lavatories.
Celeste:	He *says* he's normal.
Yusef:	He bullies people on the way home.
Mark:	He says nasty things about people's families.
Celeste:	He *says* he's normal.
Lisa:	We'd all be happier if he were –
All-the-class:	Ssshhh! Lisa! Don't say it!
Lisa:	Well, it's true!

Celeste:	But he says he's normal!
Yusef:	Well, then. If Barry Hunter's normal, I don't ever want to be normal.
Elaine:	Nor me.
Penny:	Nor me.
Lisa:	Nor me.
Stephen:	Nor me.
Mark:	Nor even me!
All-the-class:	None of us! If Barry Hunter is *normal*, we'd rather be *weird*.
Celeste:	See! Now you know what everyone thinks of you, Barry Hunter. Oh, they've all kept quiet, because they're scared, and don't want you picking on them. But out of everyone in the class, if being normal means being like you –
All-the-class:	Then nobody wants to be normal! No, thank you!
Barry:	I'll fix you Celeste. Everything around here was all right before you came. But I'll get you!
Celeste:	You'll get me when pigs fly!
Barry:	I'll stop you going to the lavatories.
Celeste:	Just try it, Bully Boots!
Barry:	All right! I will!
Celeste:	Right!
Barry:	Right!
Celeste:	Right!
Barry:	Right!

15

(Barry starts to guard the girls' lavatories. Celeste and Elaine try to walk in, arm in arm.)

Barry: I'll let Elaine go in, but I won't let you.

Celeste: Fine by me.

(Celeste and Penny try to go in, arm in arm.)

Barry: I'll let Penny in, but I won't let you.

Celeste: Fine by me.

(Celeste and Tracey try to go in, arm in arm.)

Barry: I'll let Tracey in, but I won't let you.

Celeste: Fine by me.

Half-the-class (1): He's stopping Celste from going to the lavatories!

Half-the-class (2):	And the bell's going to ring in a minute!
	(Celeste runs off.)
Half-the-class (1):	She's going off the other way now!
Half-the-class (2):	Where's she going?
Tracey:	Here's Mr Fairway. It's the bell!
Stephen:	She's going to be late!
Yusef:	Quick! Get in line.
Penny:	Where's Celeste?
	(Celeste comes on stage on the opposite side from the way she left.)
Mark:	Here she comes.
Paul:	Where's she been?
Lisa:	She went to the lavatory.
Peter:	No, she didn't. Barry Hunter's blocking it.
Lisa:	She did. *(Whispering)* She went in the *Boys'*!
All-the-class:	*(Whispering)* In the *Boys'*?
Lisa:	*(Whispering)* Celeste went in the *Boys'*!
	(Barry Hunter comes back from guarding the girls' lavatories.)
Barry:	What are you all whispering about?
All-the-class:	*(Shouting)* Celeste went in the Boys'!
Mr Fairway:	What are you all shouting about?
All-the-class:	*(Speaking normally)* Nothing. Nothing, sir. *(Then whispering again)* Have you heard the news? Celeste went in the Boys'!

17

Paul: Here comes Celeste. What's she carrying?

Tracey: A pen and a book. Show us the pen, Celeste. Oh, look! It has ten separate colours you can choose. It's even got silver and gold!

Yusef: What about the book? It has a golden cover. Is it fairy tales, Celeste?

Celeste: No.

Stephen: Is it adventure stories?

Celeste: No.

Paul: Is it Arabian Nights?

Celeste: No.

Elaine: Is it ghost stories?

Celeste: Wrong again.

Mark: Let me look. Hey! There's nothing in it! All the pages are blank.

Ian: What's the point of a book with nothing in it?

Celeste: Wait and see.

Lisa: Watch out. Here comes Barry Hunter.

All-the-class: *(In a whisper chant)*
Here comes Barry Hunter,
Making people cry.
Who's he picking on today?
Poor old Marigold.

Barry: What's that foul smell? Is it you, Marigold?

Lisa: Leave Marigold alone. You know she's too shy to stand up to you.

Barry: Sniff, sniff! It *is* you, Marigold. You smell horrible. Don't you wash?

(Marigold bursts into tears.)

Celeste:	That's it! Get in a circle, everyone! And watch me!
Lisa:	What are you going to do?
Celeste:	I'm going to write.
Lisa:	What? In your beautiful empty book?
Celeste:	That's what it's for. Now, Marigold. What did he say to you – *exactly?*
Stephen:	Marigold won't answer you.
Tracey:	Marigold's too shy to open her mouth.
Celeste:	Not today. Today's special. Come on, Marigold. Unbutton your beak. I want to write it down.
Marigold:	He 'said ... He said ... "What's that foul smell? Is it you, Marigold?"
	(Marigold bursts into tears again.)
Celeste:	Now I'm going to write the whole story down. How we were all standing here, perfectly happily, and then Barry Hunter came up and said that to Marigold and made her cry.
Yusef:	You needn't put in that it made her cry.
Celeste:	Yes, I must. I write the Truth inside the Book of Deeds. The Truth, the Whole Truth, Nothing But the Truth.
Marigold:	*(Covering her mouth with shock)* Oh!
All-the-class:	*(Chanting as if they are all under a spell)* She writes The Truth inside the Book of Deeds. The Truth, the Whole Truth, Nothing But the Truth.

Celeste:	*(Writing in the book)* "… and then poor Marigold burst into tears." There. Finished. Who wants to sign their name to be the first witness?
Stephen:	And be first to be bashed by Barry Hunter? No, thank you!
Celeste:	Nobody?
All-the-class:	No thanks, Celeste!
Celeste:	You'd get to use the wonderful pen with ten separate colours, even silver and gold …
All-the-class:	Ooooooh!
Mark:	Could I sign my name in silver?
Celeste:	Yes.

Mark:	And could I write it anywhere on the page?
Celeste:	Yes.
Mark:	And could I underline my name in gold?
Celeste:	Yes.
Mark:	All right, then. After all, Barry Hunter bashes me up almost every day, so it won't really make any difference.
Stephen:	Can I go after Mark? Can I write in purple?
Celeste:	You can.
Lisa:	Can I go after him? Write my name in pine green, and dot the *i* with the yellow?
Celeste:	Yes, you can.
All-the-class:	Me next! Me next, please!
	(They all queue up to sign the Book of Deeds.)
Celeste:	There! Lots of witnesses. He can't bash you all up.
Ian:	Not all at once!
Celeste:	Don't you worry. I promise you all, everything's going to change around here. You wait and see.
	(Celeste goes off, leaving them all staring after her.)
Marigold:	She *is* an angel. Now I'm sure of it.
Lisa:	Why?
Marigold:	Because of something that we learned in church. We all sit in a circle ... *(Everyone sits in a circle round Marigold)* ... and we are told stories. One of the stories is about an angel who is upright and strong.

22

Penny:	Celeste is upright and strong.
Marigold:	And this angel is perfect.
Ian:	Celeste's not perfect. She tripped Barry up.
Stephen:	And bit him. Hard.
Tracey:	Sssh! Let Marigold tell us.
Marigold:	And the angel stands at heaven's gate.
Mark:	Just like she stood at ours!
Marigold:	And the angel has a job. The job is to write down everything you ever did – whether it's good or bad – inside the Book of Deeds.
Lisa:	Keeping a record of everything?
Marigold:	That's right. And the angel's called the Recording Angel.
Tracey:	Is it the angel's job to tell you off?

Marigold:	Not really. But if it's a good deed, the angel smiles when she writes it down. And if it's a bad deed, she weeps.
Stephen:	Never seen Celeste weep!
Marigold:	But even the angel's tears can't wash out what is written down. Whatever the deed was, it has to stay in the book for ever and ever.
All-the-class:	*(Solemnly)* For ever and ever ...
	(There is a long silence. Then:)
Penny:	It makes me feel shivery all over!
Yusef:	Have a crisp.
Penny:	No thanks. I've stopped eating them.
Tracey:	Have a sweetie then.
Penny:	No thanks. I've stopped eating them, too.
Tracey:	If you stop eating crisps and sweets, Barry Hunter won't be able to call you Moving Mountain much longer!
Penny:	Good!
Lisa:	I think what Celeste said is already coming true. Everything's going to change around here.
All-the-class:	Good!

> *Scene 4*
>
> ***From the Staffroom Window***
> *(Starring: Headteacher, Mr Fairway, Celeste, Barry Hunter, Lisa, Stephen, Yusef, Ian, Mark, Elaine, Tracey, Marigold, All-the-class.)*
>
> *(The headteacher and Mr Fairway are standing on one side of the stage, watching the children on the other side.)*

Headteacher: What are you staring at out of that window?

Mr Fairway: I'm watching my class in the playground.

Headteacher: What can you see?

Mr Fairway: The usual. In the last twenty minutes I've seen Barry Hunter bumping everybody, and sniffing at Marigold, and stopping people going in the lavatories, and spoiling people's games.

Headteacher: Should we go down there?

Mr Fairway: They've got to learn to sort themselves out.

Headteacher: Some of them bring a lot of it on themselves.

Mr Fairway: If they stayed away from him, maybe he wouldn't bother them.

Headteacher: Nobody's parents have come up and complained.

Mr Fairway:
Headteacher: } We'll go down if it doesn't stop.

All-the-class: It doesn't stop.

Lisa: It's gone on all day. Poor Celeste's hand is *aching* from writing it all down.

Celeste: What happened next?

Stephen: Well, first he chased me round and round the lavatories, and then he stopped me getting in the only free one, and then he poked his head under the door.

Celeste: *(Writing fast)* "... poked his head under the door." Who wants to be a witness?

Yusef: Me!

Ian: Me!

Mark: Me!

(They all gather round and sign the Book of Deeds.)

Celeste: What happened next?

Elaine: Well, first he stands up in the middle of the fashion show game I've fixed up with Tracey, and he starts booing really loudly –

Tracey: So everyone felt really stupid and embarrassed and no one wanted to carry on. So the whole game was ruined.

Celeste: *(Writing fast)* " ... and so the whole game was ruined." Who wants to be a witness?

Marigold: Me!

Lisa: Me!

Tracey: Me!

(They gather round and sign the Book of Deeds.)

Celeste: What happened next?

Mark: Well, Barry Hunter kept bumping into everyone on the way to Assembly. He said "Stop bumping!" loudly to everyone he bumped, but it was him bumping, and he did it hard.

Celeste: *(Writing fast)* "... but it was him bumping, and he did it hard." Who wants to be a witness?

Ian:	Me!
Yusef:	Me!
Elaine:	Me!

(They gather round and sign the Book of Deeds.)

Celeste:	My hand's so tired, it's almost falling off.
Lisa:	The book's nearly full up already.
Celeste:	Only one page to go.
Lisa:	What happens when it's full?
Celeste:	You wait and see.
Yusef:	Oh, no! Here he comes again.

(Enter Barry.)

All-the-class: *(In a whisper chant)*
Here comes Barry Hunter,
Making people cry.
Who's he picking on today?
Poor old –

Headteacher: *(Looking out of the window again)* It hasn't stopped.

Mr Fairway: If they stayed away from him, maybe he wouldn't bother them.

Headteacher: Yes, some of them bring a lot of it on themselves.

Mr Fairway: None of their parents have complained.

Headteacher: } After all, they've got to learn to sort themselves
Mr Fairway: } out.

(The Headteacher and Mr Fairway look at one another in a very worried way.)

Scene 5

By the School Gates
(Starring: Celeste, Lisa, Elaine, Yusef, Penny, Mark, Paul, Half-the-class (1) and Half-the-class (2).)

Lisa: Where's Celeste? Why isn't she here yet?

Elaine: Maybe she's sick.

Yusef: Maybe she had to go to the dentist.

Penny: Maybe she's only late.

Mark: There's Mr Fairway, off to fetch the bell.

Lisa: Oh, please come, Celeste! Come round the corner now! Don't let us down!

Paul: What do you mean, "Don't let us down"?

Lisa: I don't know, exactly. It's just that, when Celeste's here, everything seems different somehow.

Elaine: Better.

Mark: Safer.

Penny: Nicer.

Lisa: Different.

Paul: Penny's the one who's different. Look at her.

Penny: My skirt's so loose, it's almost falling off.

Elaine:	You ought to move the button.
Penny:	No fear. I *like* it loose. I'm *happy* with it flapping.
Lisa:	See? Even Penny's happy now. That's different.
Mark:	That's because Barry Hunter can't call her Moving Mountain any more. But I can't change, can I? So he can still laugh at my glasses and my sticky-up hair and the funny way I walk. He can still call me Mark the Martian. Celeste won't manage to change that.
Lisa:	Oh, *won't* she? You wait and see!
Paul:	If she comes ...
Penny:	Oh, hurry up, Celeste!
Elaine:	There she is! I can see her!
Mark:	Here she comes.
All-the-class:	Hurry up, Celeste! Run!
	(Celeste arrives panting and spreads her hands.)
Celeste:	Disaster!
All-the-class:	What is it? What's happened?
Celeste:	Last night I cried so much I had to peg my pillow up to dry!
All-the-class:	But *why?*
Celeste:	Oh, the story's too horrible! I can hardly bear to tell you.
All-the-class:	Tell us! Tell us!
Celeste:	Well! You know I'm frightful at arithmetic.

30

All-the-class:	Yes, we know that.
Celeste:	And all those horrid black squiggles on the pages of the maths book just put me in a terrible tizzy.
All-the-class:	Yes, we know that.
Celeste:	And Mr Fairway says all the pretty things he can think of …
Half-the-class (1):	*(Imitating Mr Fairway)* "I'm sure you've nearly got it."
Half-the-class (2):	*(Imitating Mr Fairway)* "Yes, you're coming along nicely."
Celeste:	But *he* knows –
All-the-class:	And *we* know –
Celeste:	And *I* know –
All the class:	We *all* know –

Celeste:	That I'm just frightful at arithmetic! I'm worse than anyone else. And if I even ask him what page everyone else is on, he only says –
Half-the-class (1):	(*Imitating*) "Don't worry about everyone else."
Half-the-class (2):	(*Imitating*) "Just get on with your own work."
Celeste:	But I'm such a dilly, it's impossible. Trying to teach me maths is like trying to plough the sea. There isn't any point. No point at all. The poor man's tried for weeks and weeks and weeks, and still I can't add eight to eight, and make fourteen –
All-the-class:	No, *six*teen!
Celeste:	Or take two from ten, and get seven –
All-the-class:	No, *eight!*
Celeste:	Or divide twenty by four, and get six –
All-the-class:	No, *five!*
Celeste:	Or multiply twelve by four, and get forty-six –
All-the-class:	No, forty-*eight!*
Celeste:	See? It's impossible. And so I'm off.
All-the-class:	Off?
Celeste:	Off!
Lisa:	Do you mean *leaving?*
All-the-class:	*Leaving?*
Celeste:	Yes.
Penny:	How can you leave us?
Celeste:	Don't even ask me! Just thinking about it, I'm a puddle of tears!

Mark:	When are you going?
Celeste:	Almost at once. I've really just swooped in to say goodbye.
Half-the-class (1):	Oh, Celeste!
Half-the-class (2):	That's terrible.
Celeste:	Isn't it awful? I shall weep buckets. I'll sob so hard, you'll have to mop the floors behind me as I go.
All-the-class:	Oh, Celeste!

(The bell rings, and they all troop off.)

Scene 6

In the Classroom
(Starring: Mr Fairway, Mark, Barry Hunter, Celeste, Penny, Lisa, Half-the-class (1), Half-the-class (2).)

Mr Fairway: I'm just off to fetch the register, and when I come back I want to see everyone still sitting quietly at their desks.

(He goes out. At once Barry Hunter flicks Mark's woolly off the back of his chair onto the floor, and treads on it.)

Mark: Leave my woolly alone! Don't tread on it!

(Now Barry Hunter snatches Mark's pencil box, and holds it out of reach.)

Mark: And leave my pencil box alone, too! Leave *me* alone! I wasn't bothering you.

Barry: All right. Let's be friends. Shake.

Mark: No thanks. I know the way you shake hands. It hurts.

Barry: Shake, and I'll give you a sweetie.

Mark: I don't want any of your sweets.

Barry: Yes, you do.

(He grasps Mark's hand and gives his wrist a twist-burn.)

Mark: Owww!

Barry:	See! I told you I'd give you a sweetie. A big barley-twist. Have another!
	(Barry gives Mark another, harder twist-burn.)
Mark:	*(Jumping up and down, rubbing his wrist)* Owww! Owwwwww!
	(Mr Fairway comes back in.)
Mr Fairway:	Stop clattering about, Mark. Sit *down!* I thought I told everyone to stay at their desks.
Mark:	But, Mr Fairway –
Mr Fairway:	No buts, Mark! I'm sick of saying it! Stay at your desk!
Celeste:	*(Writing fast in her gold book)* "... and then Mr Fairway came back in the room, so Mark got in all the trouble and Barry Hunter didn't even own up!"
Mr Fairway:	What are you up to, Celeste?
Celeste:	I'm finishing writing the last page in the Book of Deeds.
Mr Fairway:	The Book of Deeds? What's that?
Celeste:	It's a present for you. A going-away present.
Mr Fairway:	Going away? Who's going away?
Celeste:	I am.
Mr Fairway:	But that's the saddest news! And just as you were on the verge of getting the hang of your maths!
Celeste:	Yes, such a shame. But never mind. Here's your present. And you must take very good care of it always.

(Celeste gives him the Book of Deeds.)

Mr Fairway: But this is the book that you've been writing in all term.

Celeste: That's right. And it's for you. Though you can share it with the Headteacher if you want.

Mr Fairway: But what's in it?

Celeste: Better read it and see.

(Mr Fairway opens it and flicks through the first pages.)

Mr Fairway: I shouldn't be reading this. It's just a book of tale-telling.

Celeste: But Mr Fairway, who made up the rule we shouldn't tell?

Mr Fairway: I don't know.

All-the-class: *(Shouting)* We know! The bullies did!

Celeste: And who thinks we ought to keep that rule?

Mark: Not me!

Penny: Not me!

All-the-class: And not us!

Barry: I do!

All-the-class: See? Only the bully wants to keep the rule.

Mr Fairway: You can't expect me to believe that there's a rule that's gone on for years and years and years, just because one person wants it. There must be some other people helping.

Celeste: Yes, there must.

Mr Fairway:	Well, who?
Celeste:	Yes, who?
Half-the-class (1):	(*In a whisper*) "They've got to learn to sort themselves out."
Half-the-class (2):	(*In a whisper*) "Some of them bring a lot of it on themselves."
Half-the-class (1):	(*In a whisper*) "Nobody's parents have complained."
Half-the-class (2):	(*In a whisper*) "If they stayed away from him, maybe he wouldn't bother them."
Mr Fairway:	All right. I'll read just a little bit.
	(*Mr Fairway lowers his head and reads.*)
Mr Fairway:	Oh, this is shocking! This is horrible! This is ghastly!
All-the-class:	(*In a whisper chant*) Fighting, kicking, calling names, Pushing, breaking, spoiling games ...
Mr Fairway:	Oh, this is terrible! This is awful! This is frightful!
All-the-class:	(*In a whisper chant*) Ripping woollies, hiding shoes, Locking people in the loos ... Wasting lessons, being mean, Things you've heard and things you've seen.
Mr Fairway:	Oh, this is appalling! This is disgraceful! This is enough to make an angel weep!
	(*All-the-class turn to look at Celeste who, as though by coincidence, has pulled out a frilly hanky and is blotting daintily under her eyes.*)

Mr Fairway:	Why didn't anyone tell me all this was going on?
All-the-class:	*(In a whisper chant)* Wasting lessons, being mean, Things you've heard and things you've seen.
Mr Fairway:	*(Like an echo)* Things I've heard and things I've seen ... You're right! You're right! And things will be very different from now on!
Mark:	Good!
Penny:	Good!
All-the-class:	Good!
Lisa:	See? What did I tell you? Celeste has changed everything round here now.
Mr Fairway:	It certainly looks that way.
Lisa:	Can we go with her to the gates, to wave goodbye?
Mr Fairway:	I'll give you five minutes exactly. Not a second longer! Goodbye, Celeste. And wherever you go next, just remember to tell them we all thought you were a real *angel!*
Celeste:	*(Winking)* Oh, I will indeed!

By the School Gates
(Starring: Celeste, Barry Hunter, Paul, Stephen, Yusef, Tracey, Penny, Mark, Lisa, Marigold, All-the-class.)

Stephen: It won't take a whole five minutes to say goodbye to Celeste. We can fit in a quick game of football.

Yusef: Look! Here's an old box. We'll use this.

Stephen: Kick it!

Tracey: Kick it to me!

(A football game starts with the box as a football while Celeste stands at the gates with her friends.)

Paul: To me, now!

Penny: And to me!

Barry: Kick it to me!

Penny: All right!

(Penny kicks it to Barry Hunter, who picks it up.)

Barry: Want to see a Martian goal?

(Barry puts the box upside down on Mark's head. Some of the class start giggling.)

Barry: You look exactly like a Martian now! That's how they score their goals.

Mark: *(Lifting off the box)* Is it? Is it really?

Barry: It certainly is.

(Mark jams the box down more firmly on his head, and staggers round the playgound, talking like a robot).

Mark: Look-at-me-I-am-Mark-the-Martian-playing-football-the-way-we-play-on-Mars. Watch-me-I've-scored-a-Martian-goal.

(Tracey lifts the box off his head, and boots it.)

Tracey: Quick! Yusef!

Yusef: Ready! Kick it here!

(Paul runs over to Celeste.)

Paul: It's a pity you used up the last page in your book. Never mind! I can find some paper. I'll write it down and get the witnesses.

(The game stops and everyone stares.)

Celeste: Write what down?

Paul: Didn't you see? Didn't you hear? Barry Hunter put the box on Mark's head.

Mark: But that was only a game.

Paul: Was it?

Mark: I think so. I enjoyed it.

Paul: But then he said that you looked exactly like a Martian!

Mark:	But I did. I had a box on my head. So that was only a joke.
Paul:	Was it?
Mark:	I think so. I enjoyed it.
Paul:	But that's what Barry Hunter always used to say. "Only a joke! Only a game!" And it wasn't. So how are you supposed to tell?
Mark:	I don't know. Ask Celeste.
Paul:	Celeste, what do you think? Should I find some paper and write it all down, or shouldn't I?
Celeste:	Did *everyone* have a good time?
Mark:	I did.
Barry:	So did I.
Paul:	I was all right.
All-the-class:	We all were.
Celeste:	Then there's nothing to write. Not if everyone had a good time.
Lisa:	Is that how you worked it out?
Celeste:	Yes, it was easy. If anyone was unhappy, it went in the book. If everyone was fine, then it didn't.
Paul:	Fair enough.
Mark:	I'm happy.
All-the-class:	We all are.
Celeste:	Then it's the perfect time for me to leave. *(Looking at her watch)* Good heavens! Is it that late? I must fly!

All-the-class:	We'll just stay and watch you go ...
Celeste:	Oh, what a pity you can't! Your five minutes is up exactly. Now you have to go back inside. Oh, what a shame! Never mind. I'll stand here and wave *you* all goodbye instead.
All-the-class:	Goodbye, Celeste.
Penny & Mark:	Goodbye, and thank you, Celeste!
Marigold:	Thank you. Goodbye!
Celeste:	Goodbye! Goodbye!
All-the-class:	Goodbye!

(Wistfully, All-the-class troop back into school. Only Barry Hunter lags behind until the others are all safely inside. Then he runs back.)

Barry Hunter:	Goodbye, Celeste.

(Barry Hunter and Celeste shake hands.)

Celeste:	Goodbye.

(Barry Hunter turns to go.)

Celeste:	Oh, Barry. Wait a moment.

(Barry comes back. Celeste holds up the pen with ten separate colours.)

Celeste:	Barry, I only needed the pen to write in the Book of Deeds.

(Barry looks down at his shoes, ashamed.)

Celeste:	And there won't have to be another book, will there?
Barry:	*(Looking up, and speaking firmly)* No. Not like that.

44

Celeste:	Not ever?
Barry:	Not ever!
Celeste:	Here, then. Have the pen.
Barry:	What? As a present? Just for me?
Celeste:	Yes. Though you could share it with the friends you make.
Barry:	Friends? (*He looks at the pen, and light dawns.*) Oh, yes! Friends! Oh, thank you, Celeste! Thank you!
Celeste:	Not at all.
Barry:	Goodbye, then.
Celeste:	Goodbye.

(*Barry Hunter rushes off after the others. Celeste smiles to herself and, when he's gone, gathers herself together and makes as if to take off upwards into the air. Then she seems to think better of it. She shrugs, and runs to the gates, where she stops and turns.*)

Celeste: (*Winking*) Well, goodbye!

(*Celeste slips between the gates, and disappears.*)

The Angel of Nitshill Road has been adapted from the book of the same name. It may be interesting for pupils to compare the play with the story. This could lead on to the idea of writing playscripts from stories.

Choosing Parts

The characters of Celeste, Barry Hunter, Marigold and Mark will need confident readers.

Penny and Mr Fairway will need to be fairly confident readers – in a staged production, these characters would be on stage for some time.

Less demanding parts are those of Lisa, Peter, Tracey, Stephen, Yusef, Elaine, Ian and the Headteacher.

The rest of the class can play All-the-class, and they will also need to be split into two groups to play Half-the-class 1 and Half-the-class 2.

Putting On the Play

You may wish to put on a performance of the play, rather than just reading it. The following notes are suggestions which may provide you with a starting point for your own ideas about staging a production. Obviously, the use you make of these suggestions will depend on the time and resources available to your school.

For permission to put on a profit-making performance of *The Angel of Nitshill Road*, please contact the Editorial Department, Ginn and Company Ltd, Prebendal House, Parson's Fee, Aylesbury, Bucks HP20 2QY.

(There is no need to apply for permission if you are not charging an entrance fee, but please let us know if you are putting on any performance of this play, as we would be interested to hear about it.)

Staging

The Angel of Nitshill Road is divided into seven scenes. Five of these take place in the school playground, for which minimal staging is needed. Optional background scenery might include a painted brick wall or even a set of school gates.

In **Scene 4**, 'From the Staffroom Window', Mr Fairway and the Headteacher could stand on blocks or scaffolding and look down on the other characters. If this is not possible, they could simply stand to one side of the stage in order to separate them from the others.

Scene 6 is set in a classroom. The characters could bring on tables and chairs for this scene and then take them off for **Scene 7**.

Half-the-class and All-the-class can act as a chorus, with all the pupils taking part. They will stay on stage almost throughout the play, and can sit or stand at the back or side of the stage.

Costumes

The play is easy to costume, as most of the characters can wear everyday school clothes. **Mr Fairway** and the **Headteacher** should be dressed formally. The following special costumes will also be needed.

Celeste – white dress, white socks, hair ribbon, frilly hanky, shiny shoes, watch.

Mark – glasses people will notice, a jumper that others can trample on.

Penny – a skirt that will look tight at first, and can then be made progressively looser.

Props

For **Celeste**, a book with a golden cover (perhaps Christmas wrapping paper); a fancy pen, preferably the sort that writes in a variety of colours.
For **Mark**, a pencil box.
For **Penny**, some bags of sweets and crisps.
For **Mr Fairway**, an old school register.
For use in the last scene, an old cardboard box.

Follow-up Work

Bullying is a problem that can affect any school. Verbal and physical abuse can exist in both playground and classroom, and almost everyone either witnesses it at some time or experiences it directly. Untold harm is done to many people by bullying, and victims of bullying at school can retain vivid memories of their experiences many years later.

Any follow-up work on bullying should take place in an atmosphere of trust and safety, which is important if pupils are to talk openly about their experiences.

There is a wealth of material available on bullying. Specially recommended is *Bullying: An annotated bibliography of literature and resources* by Alison Skinner (ISBN 0 86155 143 5). It is a superb guide to help you locate material on bullying, and is available from the Youth Work Press, 17-23 Albion Street, Leicester.

Discussion Points

General ideas on the issue of bullying:
- Children's own experiences of bullying.
- The responsibility of adults when bullying is going on.
- Ways of dealing with bullying.

Ideas from the play:
- What types of bullying are there in the play?
- Should the teachers have acted sooner, and what could they have done?
- How did Celeste persuade the others to write their names in the book?
- Why did people think Celeste was an angel?
- Do you think she was an angel? What are your reasons?

Drama
Hot-seating

Hot-seating is a strategy which can help pupils either to create a character or to develop greater understanding of a character in the text.
1. Put a chair at the front of the class and arange the rest of the class in a semicircle around it.
2. Choose a child to represent one of the characters in the play, and ask him or her to sit in the hot seat.
3. The rest of the class must ask the child questions, which he or she has to answer in role – in other words, as the character.

The object is to explore the characters' motivation for acting as they do. Appropriate characters from this play to be put in the hot seat include Celeste, Barry Hunter, Marigold, Mark, Penny and Mr Fairway. You could then ask them questions such as the following:
- To Barry – why do you pick on people?
- To Mark – how do you feel when Barry makes fun of you?
- To Penny – why did you decide to stop eating so many sweets?

Improvisation

Divide the class into small groups.
Allow time for the pupils to improvise
a situation to do with bullying. They
may wish to base this on a group
member's personal experience.
After the group has performed the
improvisation for the rest of the class,
discuss ways of resolving each situation.